FREE LANCE
and the
FIELD OF
BLOOD

Published in 2017 in Great Britain by
Barrington Stoke Ltd
18 Walker Street, Edinburgh, EH3 7LP

www.barringtonstoke.co.uk

First published by Hodder & Stoughton Ltd, 2003

ISBN: 978-1-78112-715-5

Printed in China by Leo

This book has dyslexia-friendly features

FREE LANCE
and the
FIELD OF BLOOD

PAUL STEWART

CHRIS RIDDELL

Barrington Stoke

1

"I'm making you an offer, sir knight," said the duke, as he stood up to leave. "An offer you can't refuse."

"No," I said, my voice quiet. "I don't suppose I can."

As he left, I slumped back in my chair. *He* was a powerful duke, *I* was only a free lance. What choice did I have?

*

And to think three days before it had all looked so promising. After a late start and an easy ride, it was late afternoon when I first

saw the castle of the duke of the Western Marches. With a twitch of the reins, I steered Jed across a broad river and up the bank on the far side. As the tournament field opened up before us, Jed pawed the ground.

"Easy, boy," I said.

I knew how he felt. Jed was a pure-bred Arbuthnot grey. Jousting was in his blood, and it had been a long time since we'd been at such a magnificent tournament.

"Welcome home, Jed," I whispered.

The tournament field was ablaze with colour. There were flags and banners. There were tents and marquees. The air was full of the sound of loud voices and a tangy mix of smells – leather, manure and a hog turning

over a fire. Yes, it felt good to be back at a
major castle tournament.

I checked out the opposition. All the usual
sorts were there. A big-headed knight – all
swagger and confidence, with a snarling

boar on his crest. A rich young nobleman
with a fine tent, four squires and a pack of
white dogs – out for some excitement on the
tournament field, while his daddy picked up
the bill. And, to my left, next to a very flashy
tent, stood a showman knight.

I had to laugh. With his trinkets and tat, he looked very grand. But I could see from the victory badges sewn on his silk flag, it was not all show – this knight knew how to handle a lance.

Further along, I came to a cluster of less grand tents which belonged to the knights from the Farmlands of the East. They were big, stout nobles. Some were quite handy with a lance, it's true – but to be honest, they were all far better at driving a plough than riding a horse.

Rich or poor, all the knights had one thing on their minds. The prize money. The winner of the tournament would take away a purse of fifty gold coins.

Fifty gold coins! That was more than you could win in a whole year of manor-house tournaments.

The place was packed. As well as the knights, there were blacksmiths and makers of armour, merchants and servants, valets and squires – and, no doubt, the pickpockets and other good-for-nothings who never fail to appear at tournaments like this one, where the ale flows freely and the pickings are rich. Close to the outer castle walls were the stables, where grooms tended to their masters' horses. One – a powerful black war

horse – caught my eye. 'Who,' I wondered, 'might own such a fine-looking beast?'

'Probably the Rich Kid,' I thought, and I patted Jed on the neck. "Looks like you've got competition too," I said.

"You there!" a high voice cried. "Where do you think you're going?"

I turned round and saw a fussy man glaring back at me. He wore red leggings, lace cuffs and collar, a tabard like a duchess's table cloth – and a *very* bad haircut. Think of a fat black pudding boiled in goose fat and you'll get the idea.

"Are you talking to me?" I asked.

"Yes, I most certainly am," he squeaked, and he flapped a roll of parchment at me. "Are you on the list? Have you wegistered?"

"Registered?" I said.

"I am the hewald," he said.

"Herald," I said.

"If you wish to compete in the jousting tournament, you must wegister with me. Dismount and pwesent yourself."

I'd met people like him before. Fussy little men who enjoyed ordering others around.

"I am a free lance," I told him. "I fight the Manor-House Tournaments."

The herald curled his top lip. "I'm afwaid you'll find a Castle Tournament much harder," he said. "You'll be up against the finest knights in the land." He looked me up and down. "I mean, are you quite sure you're good enough?"

I didn't say a word as I reached inside my saddle-bag. I was good enough all right. I'd won my last five tournaments and that gave me the right to mix it with the big boys – I showed him the certificates to prove it.

"I think you'll find everything's in order," I said.

"Yes, yes," he said, thrusting the papers back at me. He pulled a stick of charcoal from behind his ear and wrote my name at the bottom of his list.

Free Lance.

I tried to hide my grin from this fussy old pudding head, but it was no good. After all those years of jousts on village greens and at run-down manor houses, I was back at the Majors at last.

"Put your tent up over there," the herald said, and he flapped a hand towards a scrappy bit of grass full of thistles, beside the stables. It wasn't great, but at least I'd be close to Jed. "The tournament starts at midday," the herald said, then he turned away and strode off.

I lit a fire, put up my tent and was soon sitting down to a supper of "Squire's Stew" – rabbit, snared at sunrise and stewed at sunset, with wild mushrooms and herbs thrown in.

'This is the life,' I thought.

All round me, their squires waited hand and foot on the bonded knights. I wasn't jealous. Not for a moment. The bonded knights had squires to look after them, but they weren't free – all their lives they had to work for their masters. I'd lived like that before, and knew it wasn't for me.

I am a free lance. My own man.

"Are you hiring, sir?" a squeaky voice said.

I looked up to see a lanky, spotty lad with a big nose and straw-like hair standing in front of me. His jerkin was tattered and stained with left-overs from his last meal – which, from the look of it, had been eaten at least two days ago.

"I'm not sure I can afford a fine squire like you," I said.

"I'm very cheap, sir," the lad said. "All I need is me food and drink – and a share of any winnings, of course."

The lad shrugged. "I've tried all the other knights, sir, and most of them just laughed. But I'm a hard worker. I can polish your armour, groom your horse and fetch firewood. I'm very good at fetching firewood ..."

Something told me I was going to regret this. But then, the spotty kid looked as if he could do with a break.

"All right," I said, "you're hired, if ..."

"If, sir?"

"If you don't mind Squire's Stew."

"Oh, I love it, sir," he squeaked.

I handed him a plate. "What's your name, lad?"

"Wormrick," he said.

"Then tuck in, Wormrick. We've got a busy day tomorrow."

I found out just how busy soon enough. From the moment her ladyship's silver hankie fluttered down from her snow-white fingers, Jed and I were at it non-stop.

The silver hankie meant a field-of-silver joust, which is an easy affair. All you have to do is knock your opponent from the saddle. After a slow start Jed and I got into our stride, and knights, large and small, were soon dropping to the ground like bishops in buttery slippers.

The second day went even better. I knocked knight after fine, noble knight off their horses and sent them flying to the ground.

By now the crowd was getting excited.

The bets were flying, and a lot of people were making a lot of money on yours truly.

But not
me. *I* wouldn't
see a brass penny
unless I made it to the
semi-finals. That's how the Majors are – no
prize unless you win big.

On the third day, things got much harder.
Now the tournament got started when a gold
hankie dropped from her ladyship's fingers.

A field-of-gold joust is one where, after
they've knocked their opponents off their
horses, the knights engage in hand-to-hand

combat until one or the other gives up. It can get pretty nasty, but the crowds love it.

In the first round, I got the big-headed knight with the crest of the snarling boar. He went down hard, breaking his leg in three places – and he wasn't so big-headed any more.

Next up was the showman knight, and I knew I had trouble on my hands. I knocked him off

his horse on our first charge, but he sprang back to his feet like a dog with its tail on fire. The crowd roared as he set about me with his broadsword.

I bided my time and took whatever he dished out, because I knew his sort. They can't resist playing to the crowd and trying one clever move too many. Sure enough, it wasn't long before Showman danced past me with a sneaky right hand slice – and I had him! A swift uppercut with my shield and a short, sharp body-blow, and the show was over.

Later, back in my tent, Wormrick took a look at my injuries. With a bit of luck, there was nothing that some bandages wouldn't mend. I was through to the semi-finals and, as Wormrick finished fussing with me and went off to see to Jed, I pictured the opponent who would be waiting for me the next day.

Hengist was his name. He was a great brute of a fellow, bonded to the castle, and always dressed in dull grey armour. He was as grim and as hard as nails, and was well known for fighting dirty.

In the other semi-final, the Rich Kid with the black war horse had fought a series of

spectacular jousts. He was up against the Blue Knight, an unknown fighter who kept his visor down and his thoughts to himself. The Blue Knight had won with a series of lucky victories, and nobody gave him much chance of getting to the final.

Unlike me. All the smart money was on an outright victory for yours truly ...

Just then, the tent flaps opened and in walked the duke of the Western Marches. I'd seen him watching the events from the royal throne – and noticed the glint in his eyes as he'd won bet after bet on me winning. Close up, he was fatter than I'd thought. His teeth were yellow and pointed and his loose fur cloak made him look like an overfed wolfhound.

"You seem to be doing well," he barked. "People will make a lot of money if you defeat Hengist."

I nodded – it was a fair compliment. I should have known better.

But you're not going to do that," he said, his voice sharp.

"I'm not?" I said.

"No, you're going to lose," he said. His jagged teeth glinted. "But make sure it looks right. No one must suspect a thing ..."

"And why would I do this?" I asked.

A nasty smile spread out across Duke Wolfhound's fat face. "There's a purse of thirty gold coins for you now," he said, "and thirty more later, when you've taken a tumble."

"What if I don't?" I said.

The Duke's yellow eyes narrowed. "Then I shall just have to tell the herald that your documents are fake. You'll be thrown out on your ear." He sneered. "And don't think I'm joking."

I didn't. He didn't look like he made many jokes.

"It's a good offer," said the duke. "An offer you can't refuse."

"No," I said. "I don't suppose I can."

*

So there I was, slumped in my chair, with my head spinning.

Duke Wolfhound wanted me to cheat – to throw the joust! Me, Free Lance, throw a joust! I've never thrown a joust in my life!

I admit – the offer was tempting. I'd make more by *losing* the tournament than I would by *winning* it.

And, as a free lance, a purse of gold wasn't to be sniffed at. Then again, there was the matter of honour. Even if no one ever discovered what I had done, *I* would know ...

Just then, the tent flaps opened for a second time, and a tall, slim figure dressed in a long hooded cape stepped in.

"We must speak at once, sir knight," a voice said – a *woman's* voice. "It is a matter of the utmost importance."

2

Call me a fool, but I've always had a soft spot for a damsel in distress.

"How can I help?" I asked her.

"I ... I hardly know where to begin," she murmured.

"You could start by taking off your hood," I said.

With a snow-white hand, she pulled off her hood. Her hair was a mass of glossy red ringlets, and two dazzling emerald-green eyes full of tears stared at me.

It was her ladyship – the one who'd dropped the hankies at the tournament. She looked as if she could do with a hankie now. I gave her mine, and she used it to dab her eyes. Then she held it out to me.

"Keep it," I said. "Now, what's this all about? Shouldn't you be up at the castle getting ready for this evening's banquet?"

"Oh, sir knight," her ladyship cried. "You've got to help me! I beg you! You hold my future in your hands."

"I do?" I said.

"I followed my uncle here," she said. "I knew he was up to no good, and when I heard ..." Her face crumpled and the tears began streaming down her face again.

"Calm yourself, your ladyship," I said.

"I ... I heard him make you an offer," she sobbed. "He promised you extra money if you threw the tournament. But you must not listen to him," she begged.

"No?" I said.

"I know my uncle," she said. "He's set this whole thing up. And it's not the first time. He holds a tournament and waits for a champion like you to turn up. Everyone bets on the champion, but my uncle puts *his* bet on someone else, a knight who works for *him*. And then he makes the champion an offer he can't refuse ... That way, my uncle pays off the champion, but wins all the money from the bets for himself."

"Someone who works for *him*," I said. "Who could that be?"

Her ladyship shuddered. "Hengist," she said, her voice full of disgust. "That's who. And what's more," she whispered, "if Hengist *does* win ... then ... Oh," she said with a sob, "my uncle has promised him my hand in marriage. It doesn't matter that Hengist is brutal and cruel, only that he is loyal – and I'll be his reward for that loyalty."

"But what's this got to do with me?" I asked.

"Everything, brave sir knight!" she said.

I liked "brave". I was listening hard now.

"I have come here to beg you not to lose the joust tomorrow," she said. "If you defeat Hengist, and I know you can, then he will be disgraced. My uncle will punish him by calling off our marriage." She fluttered her eyelashes. "And you will have saved a helpless maid from a fate worse than death."

I tried to look as if I didn't care. "What's to stop your uncle marrying you off to another of his henchmen instead?" I asked.

"I won't allow that to happen," her ladyship said. "Even now, the man I love is planning our escape. But our escape will fail if Hengist gets his brutal hands on me tomorrow. So you see, I need your help," she said. "*Bold* sir knight, *brave* sir knight ..."

She was pressing all the right buttons now, but I was in a pretty pickle, and I knew it. If I threw the joust, then this beautiful girl would end up married to Hengist the Henchman. If

I didn't, the duke would be after me. I'd find myself chucked out of the tournament faster than a steaming chamber-pot from a bedroom window.

Thing is, I'm a sucker for a pretty face, and faces don't come much prettier than her ladyship's.

"Don't worry," I heard myself say. "Whatever happens tomorrow, I give you my word as a knight that Hengist won't lay a finger on *you*."

Her ladyship squeezed my hand. "I knew I could count on you, dear, *sweet* knight."

And with that, she turned and hurried away. I smiled after her stupidly. My promise was ringing in my ears. What *was* I going to do tomorrow?

Just then, Wormrick's messy hair and spotty face appeared at the tent flap. He was out of breath and, when he spoke, his voice was high and squeaky. "The horses are all jittery, sir," he said. "Something's spooked them."

"Rats, perhaps," I suggested. "Or maybe a snake. I'd better look. The last thing I need is something happening to Jed, along with everything else."

"Everything else?" Wormrick said.

"You don't want to know, Wormrick," I said. "Come. To the stables."

The sound of troubled whinnying and neighing greeted us from the stables. The horses had been spooked all right.

As we came close, a tall, raven-haired beauty stepped out of the shadows. She stopped when she saw us.

"I'm looking for my mistress," she said, fixing me with her dark eyes. "I am the lady of the castle's maid and I need to find her."

"You won't find her in there," said Wormrick. "That's the stables."

The maid shot him an evil look.

"Your mistress has returned to the castle," I said. "Now, if you'll excuse us, I have a horse to look after."

The maid had the flicker of a smile on her lips as she stepped back to let us pass.

In the stables, the horses were all skittering around, stamping their hoofs and tossing their heads. The Rich Kid's black war horse had broken out of its stall and was rearing up, pawing the air with its front legs. Its eyes were rolling and glistening froth dripped from the sides of its mouth.

I pushed past a squire – who was hopping about from one leg to the other – and approached the panicky horse. I kept my arms wide and talked sweet-nothings in a low, calm voice. The horse snorted and backed away, but I could tell by the way its ears twitched that it was listening to me.

"Easy, now," I murmured. "Nobody's going to hurt you."

Its eyes stopped rolling and, when I patted its neck, it turned and licked my hand. I've always had a way with horses. I only hoped Jed wasn't getting jealous.

The squire stepped forward. "Thank you, kind sir," he said. "All the horses have been terrible jumpy. Maybe the hay's gone sour ..."

I looked round. The horses' drinking trough had been knocked over and the wooden stall was smashed and in splinters.

"Maybe," I said. "Still, the horses seem all right now." I turned to the war horse. "Eh, boy?" I said.

The horse gave a soft whinny and blew warm air into my face.

"Hey, you," a snooty voice said. "What do you think you're doing with my horse?"

I turned, to find the Rich Kid standing before me, his hands on his hips. He was dressed in fancy clothes, ready for the banquet no doubt. There were swirls of silver thread on his coat, and a buckle of gold and rubies on his belt. That outfit must have cost his daddy a pretty penny!

Our eyes met.

"What *are* you?" he sneered. "A squire? A *serf*?"

"He's a knight," Wormrick spat. "And he just calmed your horse down. If he hadn't come to help, your poor horse would have broken its legs."

"Knight, eh?" the Rich Kid said, looking me up and down. "Sorry, old chap, I didn't know. You don't look much like a knight to me ..." He gave my patched tunic and old boots a look of disgust. "You've got to admit, it's an easy mistake to make."

I didn't answer back – even though I knew Wormrick wanted me to. Then the Rich Kid turned on his own squire.

"What have you to say for yourself, eh?"

"P ... please, sir," the terrified squire stammered. "One minute your horse was fine, the next I couldn't do a thing with him, and ..."

"I don't have time for all this now," the Rich Kid interrupted. "Some of us have banquets to go to."

"Yes ... S ... sorry, sir," said the squire.

"Rub him down and settle him in another stall," the Rich Kid called back as walked away.

"And if he gets troublesome again, take the whip to him."

I snorted. "Best way to ruin a good horse."

The Rich Kid spun round. "When I want your advice, sir knight, I'll ask for it," he snapped.

"Free lances," he muttered as he strode out. "Scum of the tournaments."

Rich Kid was certainly pushing his luck, and I'd have liked to teach him a lesson he wouldn't forget. But this wasn't the time or the place. Sometimes, in my line of work, a thick skin is far better than a quick temper. There would be time to teach Rich Kid better manners on the jousting field.

I crossed the stable to where Jed was tethered. He seemed fine. I patted him, nuzzled my face against his, and told him he was the finest horse a knight could wish for. Wormrick came up behind me.

"When you've quite finished," he said with a laugh, "Jed needs his supper. And *you've* got a banquet to go to, remember."

"You're right, Wormrick," I said. I pulled some bits of straw from my hair, brushed myself down and turned to face him. "How do I look?" I asked.

Wormrick grinned. "Not bad for a free lance," he said.

That was good enough for me. "See that Jed is fed and watered, and help yourself to supper in the tent," I told him as I set off.

"And get a good night's sleep."

"I will, sir," Wormrick squeaked.

It was an honour to dine inside the castle itself, and I *had* made it to the semi-finals – but I didn't feel excited or proud. Instead, as I clattered over the drawbridge, I couldn't get her ladyship's emerald-green eyes out of my mind. Nor could I forget the sound of the duke's voice making me an offer I couldn't refuse.

3

I grabbed the heavy handles of the doors to the great hall, and pushed them open. As I stepped inside, a blast of heat, noise and smell struck me like a hammer blow.

The hall was tall and grand, with flags fluttering from the high ceiling and fresh straw on the floor. To my right, a great fire blazed. There were pillars decorated with ivy and at the top of the hall was a table where the duke and her ladyship sat.

I was late, that much was clear. All round me, the banquet was in full swing, with the knights and squires at the long tables shouting as they tucked into their bread and stew and supped their penny ale.

There were musicians in the gallery playing jolly tunes. There were jugglers and tumblers and a person on stilts, all performing on the straw-covered floor – and taking care not to step on the huge, grey hounds that lay about, gnawing on the mutton bones that their masters tossed to them.

The jester was making the most noise of all. He was a tiny fellow with bells on his hat and a voice more shrill than a princess caught on the privy. He was jumping about on a hobby horse, with a rough wooden

sword in his hand, acting out some kind of
mock-battle with a snappy terrier dressed up
as a dragon ...

"Your name, sir?" someone shouted at me.

I turned to see a page with a roll of
parchment in his hands. He looked me up and
down with a sniff.

"I'm probably on your list as Free Lance," I
replied.

For a moment the page scanned the parchment. When he spotted my name, his eyebrows shot upwards.

"Oh, yes, indeed, sir," he said. "Follow me, sir."

I went with him, between the rows of knights and squires and towards the high table at the far end of the hall. Some of them turned from their bread and stew and raised their tankards to me. Others cheered.

"Fine jousting, sir knight!" someone cried, and the cheers grew more rowdy.

I nodded and kept on walking. I was aware of Duke Wolfhound's eyes on me. The page led me to stand before the top table and I bowed low.

Duke Wolfhound – face flushed and fangs glinting – lifted his goblet to me. "Eat, drink and make merry, sir knight," he said. "You have an important day tomorrow."

I nodded. "Thank you, sir," I said. "Indeed I have."

The duke threw back his head and roared with laughter, as if I had just told him the most hilarious joke. To his left, Hengist – a huge leg of lamb in his hand – leaned across and whispered something into the duke's ear, which made him laugh even louder.

The page led me on towards my seat. As I passed her ladyship, seated to the duke's left, she stared at me, her emerald eyes full of tears.

Don't forget, she mouthed silently.

Forget? There was no chance of me forgetting what she'd told me. Not forgetting was easy. It was deciding what to do about it that was much more difficult.

I took my place. To my right was a large woman in dull clothes, and next to her was the Rich Kid. He was waving away a platter of meat like the spoilt brat that he was, and demanding a flagon of the finest wine. I turned away in disgust. To my left was an empty seat.

"Who's meant to be sitting there?" I asked a page, as he filled my tankard with thick ale.

"The Blue Knight, sir," he replied. "But he's been keeping himself to himself all tournament."

I nodded. The Blue Knight's jousting skills were dismal. And so I wasn't surprised that he'd hit on the gimmick of being mysterious to keep the crowds interested. He'd had some lucky victories – opponents' horses bolting or flinging their riders from the saddle. Even so, he *had* ended up in the semi-finals. And that was no fluke.

"What would sir care to start with?" asked another page.

He offered me salmon and trout, pâtés and truffles, and larks' tongues in quivering jelly.

"I think I'll try a little bit of everything," I said.

The two pages leaped into action. I tucked in. Everything tasted even better than it looked – apart from the larks' tongues in jelly, which I threw to the dogs.

The second course was even more amazing. We had pigs with apples in their mouths, peacocks roasted in their own feathers, hens and pheasants, and silver platters of slices of meat, dripping with sauces. The pages saw to my every need, slicing and serving, and never allowing my tankard to get less than half full.

I would have rather eaten in silence, but the woman to my right, who I found out was the

duke's aunt, wouldn't stop talking. She talked
of the weather, of the seasons, of her relatives,
of her prayers and of duty. She talked of the
fresh straw and the bright candles – and, of
course, of the jester.

"His act is *so* boring." She yawned. "We've
seen this George and the Dragon business so
many times before."

I nodded, but made no reply. She didn't
seem to notice, but kept on talking – now all
about the colours of the flags hanging above
our heads, and how red did so clash with
green.

I looked round. The
Rich Kid was tossing lumps
of meat to his white
wolfhounds. Hengist and
Duke Wolfhound were
deep in conversation.

Her ladyship sat staring straight ahead, not touching her food. With her was the raven-haired maid I'd met in the stables. When two of the white wolfhounds got into a nasty fight over a scrap of meat, the maid looked over at the Rich Kid with a sneering grin on her face.

"Ah, now this is more like it," the Duke's aunt said, and she nudged me in the ribs. "The troubadour."

I looked round and saw a tall young fellow, dressed in simple clothes, walk to the front of the gallery and start to strum his lute. Everyone in the hall fell silent. The troubadour burst into song.

"My Lords and Ladies, listen well," he sang, his voice – like all troubadours, I thought – far too high. He sounded like a knight whose leggings were too tight. He made his way down the stairs. *"I have a tale of chivalry to tell ..."*

Beside me, the Duke's aunt sighed longingly and closed her eyes. The knights on the low tables seemed just as spellbound. But I'd heard it all before – endless tales of sweet damsels and wicked villains, and a knight in shining armour who arrives to put everything right.

Life just wasn't that simple. And I should know – even if there were some people who believed that it was. I turned to look at her ladyship.

I was surprised at the look on her face. She was gazing at the troubadour as he crossed the hall. Her eyes were wide open and her face shone. Her lips were softly parted and her eyes gleamed with excitement.

"So *that's* the man she loves!" I groaned. If she was in love with a troubadour, then she was in more trouble than I thought.

I continued my meal, deep in thought. Her ladyship had been promised to a great hulk of a knight but she was in love with a troubadour. He wouldn't be much help! No wonder she needed *my* help. The troubadour didn't look as if he'd be much good if it came to any rough stuff, and he probably didn't have two brass pennies to call his own. My heart went out to the young lovers.

Life could be complicated and difficult all right.

The song finished and Duke Wolfhound climbed to his feet and lifted his goblet of wine high in the air.

"Sir knights, one and all!" he bellowed. "A toast to our semi-finalists! May the best man win!"

"May the best man win!" the crowd roared back.

Beside me, the Duke's aunt tapped me on the arm. "I have so enjoyed our little chat," she said. "Good luck tomorrow, sir knight."

I nodded and smiled. But I knew that the only luck I'd have was what old Duke Wolfhound allowed me.

4

The sun was high in the sky as Jed and I made our way across the tournament field. I could tell by the way he tossed his head and pawed the ground that he was keen to get started. As for me, it was another story. I felt rubbish! My arms and legs were heavy, my chest hurt and my head felt as if it had been stuffed with goose feathers.

The trouble was, I was worn out. I hadn't slept a wink all night. I just couldn't stop thinking about the fix I was in.

Should I throw the joust, as Duke Wolfhound wanted, and walk away with a heavy purse? Or should I fight fair and save her ladyship, but risk a heavy beating from Wolfhound's thugs? My head said one thing and my heart said another. I lay awake all night trying to choose. The early-morning light was streaming in through the holes of my tent when I decided at last what to do.

I wasn't proud of myself, I can tell you. What I'd decided went against every knightly bone in my body. I hated to do it, but there was nothing else for it. I would go down to Hengist – I'd let him defeat me.

Of course, I'd make it look good. I'd flip from Jed's back and, taking care not to hurt myself, land on the ground in a clatter of armour and a cloud of dust – but then stay down ...

Afterwards, I'd collect the gold that Duke Wolfhound had promised me. Then I'd tell him to let her ladyship go, or I'd shop him – I'd tell the herald that the duke had asked me to lose on purpose. That would bring an end to Duke Wolfhound's days as a fixer of tournaments.

If Hengist had a problem with that, we could have a nice little chat about it, away from the tournament field. I'd also decided that I'd give her ladyship half the gold so that she and the troubadour could travel far away and live happily ever after.

As plans went, it wasn't great.

I couldn't be sure that the herald would take my side and challenge the duke. Hengist might prove a bit of handful, and her ladyship might end up at the top of a tall tower with no staircase. But all in all, it was the best I could come up with.

Just then, a trumpet sounded and I looked round to see the herald waddle to the centre of the field. The first joust was about to begin.

"At the south end, in wed and white stwipes," the herald called out, "I give you bwave Sir Walph of Mountjoy!"

That was the Rich Kid and the crowd cheered.

"At the north end," the herald continued. "Dwessed in blue, the ... errm ... the Blue Knight!"

The cheers grew louder. Everyone loves an underdog.

The herald raised his arms. The crowd fell silent. All eyes turned to the grandstand where the duke and her ladyship sat. Her ladyship stood up and let a glittering hankie flutter down over the balcony. It landed on the grass.

The herald inspected it. "Let the field-of-gold joust begin!" he cried.

At the second trumpet blast, the Rich Kid spurred his black war horse on with a harsh kick. The animal sprang forward, its ears flat, its muzzle foaming, the whites of its eyes glinting as it tossed its head. It looked wild and angry – like a creature possessed.

I saw that the raven-haired maid was standing behind her ladyship. Her eyes were fixed on the horse and rider.

At the other end of the field, I saw the Blue Knight digging his heels into his horse. It was all skin and bone. I shook my head. I didn't know who the Blue Knight was, but he wasn't a natural jouster. He rode like a country bumpkin, and he couldn't hold his lance steady to save his life. Things were looking pretty bad for him and the Rich Kid was just getting into his stride now.

The Rich Kid had his war horse on a tight rein. He levelled his lance to target the Blue Knight. It was a lovely move, one even *I* would have been proud to perform. The Blue Knight didn't stand a chance.

At least, that was what I thought. But at that moment, an amazing thing happened. Just as the two knights were about to clash,

the black war horse let out a terrible screech, arched its back and crashed headlong into the tournament turf, pitching the Rich Kid high up in the air – and onto the Blue Knight's wavering lance.

There was the crunch of bones shattering, the splintering of wood, and a shuddering crash as the Rich Kid hit the ground. He didn't move. The herald strode across the field and poked the crumpled body with his toe.

"Victowy!" he cried and raised his arm. "The Blue Knight will go into the final."

The crowd seemed confused. Only a couple of feeble cheers rose above the murmur. No one could quite believe what they'd seen. For a healthy war horse simply to collapse like that was unheard of.

The Rich Kid's four squires rushed up and fussed about their master. I was more concerned about the stricken war horse. I got down from Jed, strode over and kneeled down beside the poor creature. It whimpered, one wild eye staring back at me. There was blood at its mouth, and its front legs were broken.

"There, there, boy," I said. There was
nothing I could do.

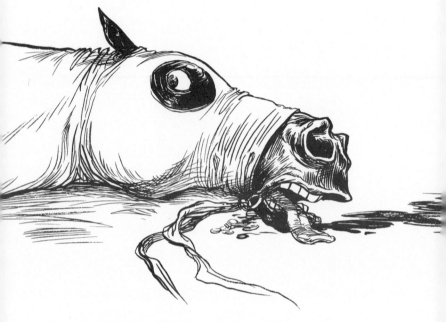

I looked up to see a man-at-arms
approaching with a crossbow. I knew that
an arrow between the eyes was the kindest
thing for the horse, but I still couldn't watch. I
turned away.

"Come, come, sir knight, it is time," said
voice that I knew, and I felt old pudding-head,
the herald, tug at my arm.

"Sad of course that the horse must be put down," he said, "but these things happen."

I nodded. He was right of course. As he led me away, I saw the raven-haired maid staring hard at me. I looked away, shocked by the thin smile on her lips.

"Huwwy up," the herald said. "The joust must begin without further delay."

I climbed onto Jed's back and took my place at the south end of the tournament field.

We waited as the war horse was dragged off, and the Rich Kid – who was moaning softly now – was taken off on a stretcher. A ripple of excitement ran through the crowd. I nodded to those who were cheering me on and raised my head proudly. I would enjoy those cheers while they lasted.

I, a free lance, had made it to the semi-finals of a major castle tournament. It was only a shame that, on the second tilt, I would have to go down as hard as the Rich Kid had just done – and the cheers would turn to boos when the crowd saw that I wasn't getting up and their favourite, the knight they'd bet so much on, had lost.

At the other end of the field, Hengist had mounted his stallion. He cut an impressive figure, even in his dull grey armour. But he was too slow and plodding to be a great jouster. At least, that was what I hoped.

As the trumpet sounded, the herald stepped forward. "At the north end, we have Sir Hengist of the Western Marches."

There were both boos and cheers as the crowd greeted the local boy.

"At the south end," the herald went on, "Sir ... um ... Fwee Lance."

For a second time that afternoon, all eyes turned to look at her ladyship. She stood and held the hankie high. As our eyes met, an uncertain smile fluttered across her face. I pulled down the visor of my helmet.

The hankie fell.

"Let the field-of-gold joust begin!" cried the herald.

With a loud snort, Hengist spurred his horse. I twitched Jed's reins, and he was off. Beneath me, I could feel his pounding hoofs gathering speed. How he loved the tournaments – the charged air in his nostrils, the boiling blood pumping in his body.

I lifted my shield, fixed my sights on Hengist, and levelled my lance. The great oaf was lumbering towards me. He was all brawn

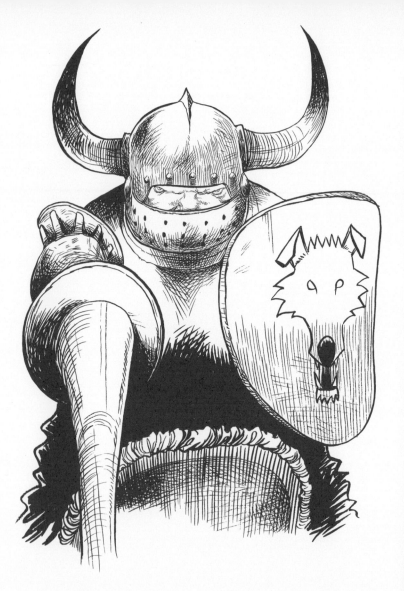

and no brain, bouncing about in his saddle like a barrel of ale in an ox-cart. His great heavy armour was pitching him this way and that.

When I was a lance-length away, I saw he was leaning forward so heavily that he'd left his neck wide open to attack. I could have finished him off there and then. Instead, I turned my lance away, and took a blow to my shield from Hengist as he and his horse thundered past.

The crowd gave a loud gasp of surprise.

On the second joust, as we drew close to one another, I dropped my shoulder and lifted my shield to give Hengist a target that even a hopeless jouster like him couldn't miss. I urged Jed on and shifted my lance round so that it would strike his armour without hurting him. Then, at the last possible moment, I slipped my feet from the stirrups and got ready for the heavy blow that I knew was about to come.

The blow came as Hengist's lance struck the top of my breast plate. A cry went up

from the crowd and the air was full of the
sound of shattering wood. I shot from the
saddle like a fish speared in the moat.

I hit the ground hard, and rolled over and
over, my armour clattering like a an iron
bucket on cobble stones. If I had to go down,
the least I could do was put on a show. I came
to rest just near the grandstand – a nice
touch, I thought – and lay there, stock still.

It was all over.

Through my visor, I glimpsed the shocked face of her ladyship looking down at me, the colour gone from her cheeks. Beside her, Duke Wolfhound grinned a nasty grin. He knew he'd won.

Just then, I felt a fierce stabbing pain in my arm where Hengist's lance had struck. I'd felt the blow of a blunt tournament lance many times before – a dull throbbing pain. This was different. I put my hand up – and was shocked to feel the end of a shattered lance shaft still there.

I pulled myself up as the crowd shouted and cheered – and tugged at the bit of splintered wood stuck in my arm.

What had hit me was not a wooden lance but the iron tip of a war lance.

I'd been taken for a fool! A total fool! The duke had never meant me to throw the joust – and lose. He'd only wanted me off my guard so that great hulk Hengist could finish me off for good. If I hadn't ridden so well, and faked a fall, I'd be dead by now.

A red mist came down. I was gripped by rage. I was ready to *kill*.

I jumped to my feet, and as I drew my sword, the crowd gave a roar like thunder.

Hengist was lumbering towards me, his own broadsword gripped in his great ham of a hand. I threw myself at him, meeting his uppercut with a high parry.

Our swords clashed, and I felt as if a red hot poker was boring into my arm. With a roar of pain, I dummied a high sword cut

to his right, but swung low instead. It was
an old trick, but it worked. My broadsword
sliced into the back of Hengist's knees and he
crashed to the ground, with a bellow like a
wounded bear.

I stood over him, my sword raised high,
about to bring it crashing down, when I felt a
hand on my arm. It was the herald.

He smiled at the crowd but whispered to me out of the corner of his mouth. "There seems to have been a slight mix-up with the lances," he said. "Most unfortunate, but we don't want it to get out of hand, do we?"

The red mist was lifting, and I felt very tired all of a sudden.

"After all," the herald said, "this is a field of gold, *not* a field of blood, wemember."

I lowered my sword. My head was swimming and my arm hurt more than ever.

"My lords, ladies and gentlemen," the herald announced in a loud voice, "Fwee Lance is into the final!"

5

Her ladyship stared down at me, her eyes brimming with tears of happiness and thanks. Beside her, Duke Wolfhound's face told a different story. With his eyes ablaze and his fangs bared, he looked like a dog in a bear pit.

He clicked his fingers and two beefy henchmen came to his side. He gave them a whispered command and they clattered down the grandstand steps and lumbered on to the tournament field. They took their broadswords out and pointed them at me.

Things were not looking good. Then something odd happened. As the two henchmen came closer, I heard a rising swell of noise and turned to see a crowd of fans burst through the rope fence. They pushed Duke Wolfhound's henchmen aside, seized me and lifted me up high. They carried me off, cheering and chanting my name as they went.

"Free Lance! Free Lance!"

It was little wonder I was so popular. Most of the crowd had bet on me and were happy to collect their winnings.

Everyone was laughing and cheering and clapping me on the back. Everyone, that is, except Duke Wolfhound.

I could see him scowling at me. With a wave of his hand, he called off his henchmen. There was nothing they could do. At least, not for now. But I knew the matter wouldn't stop there. Duke Wolfhound wasn't the sort to forgive and forget. The cold look on his face told me it wasn't his pride that was hurting him – it was his purse.

The crowd carried me round the field three times, before they trooped back to my tent. Wormrick came across to greet me.

"Well done, sir!" he said. "I knew you could ..." He gasped.

"Sir!" he cried. "You're bleeding!"

In the excitement, I'd clean forgotten about my injury. It all

came flooding back. The lance blow. The pain.
The blood ... I looked down at my breast plate.
It was dripping with the stuff.

Blood doesn't bother me. I've seen my
fair share of brave knights cut down on
the battlefield, but this was different. This
was *my* blood – and lots of it! Wormrick's
face swam before my eyes and my head felt
heavier than a lead weight.

A black sea opened up before me – and I
dived straight in.

*

I opened my eyes and tried to focus. Slowly,
the blurred shapes in front of me sharpened
into a smiling mouth and two emerald-green
eyes.

"You're awake," her ladyship said, her
voice breaking with relief. "Thank goodness. I
was fearing the worst."

"Your ladyship," I said and I sat up.

Straight away, I wished I hadn't. Pain burned into my arm like a red-hot poker.

"Easy now," her ladyship said. "Lie back again, sweet sir knight. Let me dress your wound."

I did as I was told, and sank back into the soft pillows and mattress. It was like floating on a cloud.

"Where am I?" I asked.

"You're in one of the servants' rooms in the castle," she said as she spread a thick, green paste on my arm. I almost expected to hear the hiss of steam as the wound cooled. "I had you brought here because it wasn't safe for you to return to your tent. My uncle's men are looking for you."

I nodded.

"But you have done me a great service, sir knight," she went on, "and I want to do everything I can to make sure you come to no harm." She put a bandage round me up as she spoke. "Your injuries are not too bad, but you must rest."

"Rest!" I exclaimed. "But the tournament ... The *final*!"

"That's not till tomorrow," her ladyship said firmly. "So be a good knight, lie back, and let your wounds heal. Besides," she added, "there are others far worse off than you." A smile plucked at the corners of her mouth. "Sir Hengist for one," she said. "My uncle's washed his hands of him and sent him packing."

"So the wedding's off," I said with a grin. "Good job I didn't splash out on a wedding present."

"You've done plenty for me already," she replied, returning my smile as she tied the bandage under my arm. "Thanks to you, my plans are complete. Tomorrow, when the tournament is over, I shall leave my uncle's castle for ever."

"I wish you luck, your ladyship," I said. "It can be a harsh world beyond a castle's walls."

"Luck has nothing to do with it," she said, her green eyes gleaming. "My beloved has arranged everything. He has two fine, strong horses waiting, and has bribed the castle gate-keeper with his last two gold crowns. It might be a harsh world, but with him at my side I can face anything." She smiled and planted a kiss on my forehead. "And it's all thanks to you, sweet sir knight."

"Don't mention it," I said, as I lay back against the soft pillows, still feeling the touch of her lips on my forehead.

Her ladyship put the blankets straight. "All done," she said. "Now, I must prepare myself for this evening's banquet. It wouldn't do to turn up late. My uncle mustn't suspect a thing." She squeezed my hand. "Rest here, sir knight, until you feel better."

With that, she turned and skipped from the room, as if she had not a care in the world. I hoped it would all work out for her. I'd done all I could. Now it was up to that troubadour of hers. I could only pray, for both their sakes, that he was up to the task. I had plenty of cares of my own right now.

But I couldn't risk staying in bed a moment longer – however comfy it might be. When the duke's men found my tent empty, I knew they would try to get to me through Jed or Wormrick. I had to get back to them, and make sure they were all right.

With a sigh, I slipped out from under the warm blankets. I shivered in my patched leggings and bare feet, and looked round the room for the rest of my clothes. I only hoped her ladyship hadn't sent them to the castle laundry.

At the end of the room stood a wooden screen, and I could see the edge of a mirror and the corner of a chair sticking out behind it. With a bit of luck, I'd find my missing clothes there as well.

I padded across the floor and looked. And there they were, all folded up neatly on the chair. It was the first bit of good luck I'd had all day. I slipped the jerkin over my head, hung the sword around my waist and had just sat down to pull on my boots when I heard someone enter the room.

I froze. Had the duke's henchmen found me after all?

I gripped my sword and leaned slowly forward in the chair to peer round the edge of the screen. There *was* someone in the room. But it was no henchman. Instead, I found myself looking at her ladyship's raven-haired maid. She had something in her hand – a small bottle or jar – and she was taking out the stopper as she made her way across the room.

The next moment, when she saw that my bed was empty, she stamped her foot and her eyes darted around the room. There was something about her dark look that made me decide to stay hidden. I shrank back into the shadows behind the screen and waited. The next moment there came a voice.

"So," it said, "looks like her ladyship's guest has escaped." I edged forwards and peered through a gap in the screen, to see the troubadour walk into the room.

"And he's gone before you had a

chance to weave your magic on him," he said. "How very unfortunate."

The maid tossed her black hair and narrowed her eyes. "You do your job," she said in a voice of ice. "And I'll do mine."

"Oh, don't you worry about me," said the troubadour. He strummed on his lute as he sat down on the bed and put his feet up. "You keep knocking them down, and I'll keep taking the glory."

The maid's hands flew to her hips. "If that was *all* you were doing, it would be fine," she hissed. "But I swear you're turning into her ladyship's lapdog. You trail after her the whole time, with your tongue hanging out ..."

The troubadour threw back his head and laughed. Then he put his lute down, jumped to his feet and went to take the maid in his arms.

"Get off me!" she screeched, and scratched at his face with her sharp nails.

The troubadour grabbed her by the wrists before she could do any damage. "Put away your claws," he said. "I'm only play-acting." He smiled. "You know I only have eyes for you, my dark-haired little witch."

I saw the maid relax and smile. "I can never stay angry with you for long," she said and shuddered. "It's this place. The sooner we leave, the better."

84

The troubadour nodded. "It's a great shame that brave Free Lance is not here," he said. "It would have made things so much easier."

"It doesn't matter. I'll take care of the free lance," the maid said. She hitched up her long dress and hurried over to the door. "Just make sure you're not too busy 'play-acting' when I do," she called back.

The troubadour sat back down on the bed and picked up his lute. He started strumming and singing in that rich, honey voice of his that all the ladies so loved.

"*My love has eyes of emerald green ...*" He paused and chuckled. "Or should that be, *My love has hair of raven-black ...?*"

All of a sudden, he stopped playing, jumped to his feet and tucked his lute under his arm.

"Best be off," he said. "After all, a banquet isn't a banquet without a troubadour."

As he left the room, I pulled on my boots at last, buckled up my armour and stepped out from behind the screen. My arm hurt, but it was the least of my worries. I didn't know what the troubadour and the maid were up to, but it looked as if they wanted me out of the way. And if her ladyship thought she could trust the troubadour, she was making a big mistake. I hated to be the one to break the bad news, but at least it could wait for the time being.

Right now, I had to get to Wormrick and Jed. In the meantime, her ladyship could enjoy what she thought was her last banquet – the Final Banquet.

I wasn't planning on going to the banquet – not after the day I'd just had. No, I planned to be as big a mystery as the Blue Knight. There would be *two* empty seats at the high table that evening.

I played the old toss-a-stone trick to distract the guard at the gate. Then I slipped away from the castle and darted off between the tents back to where Jed and Wormrick were. I kept to the shadows, my head down and eyes on the look-out for any sign of danger.

Ahead of me was the patch of thistles where the poor knights like me had put up their tents. I saw at once that something was very wrong.

6

There were two burly oafs dressed in Duke Wolfhound's colours standing outside my tent, flaming torches in their hands. They were waiting for someone – me. It didn't take a genius to work that one out.

The bigger of the two oafs was enormous and had cropped red hair. When he saw me, an ugly smile spread across his blotchy face.

"Just the knight we've been looking for," he sneered and nudged his friend, a pasty-faced oaf with a scar down one cheek.

Scar Face smiled. "That's right," he agreed. "You see," he said to me, "there's been an unfortunate accident."

"Accident?" I said.

"Yes, sir knight," said Scar Face. "A fire." He held the torch to the tent-flap. With a crackle and a puff of smoke, a sheet of blazing yellow leaped up the side of my tent.

"Tut tut," said Ginger as he took a great club from his belt. "First your tent burns down, and then you have a nasty fall."

"I do?" I said. My hand gripped the handle of my sword.

"That's right," said Scar Face. "A very nasty fall. Two broken legs, I believe."

I drew my sword as Ginger came for me. The heavy club whistled past my ear. He wasn't trying to break my legs – it was a crushed skull he was after.

I stepped to one side and drove the handle of my sword hard into the pit of his stomach. As he fell, I gave him a crushing blow to the back of the head. The great oaf crashed to the ground.

"Sweet dreams," I muttered.

One down, one to go. I spun round to see Scar Face, a club raised above his head, about to brain me. I swung my sword in a low, slashing cut that drew a red line across the blue and white pattern on his chest. It was just a flesh wound, but it did the trick.

Scar Face dropped his club and let out a long, loud squeal, like a greasy runt at a

pig-catching contest. I took a step forward. But he'd clearly had enough. He turned on his heels and he fled without a backward look.

I put away my sword. My tent was now fully ablaze, the fire eating away at the tent cloth like a mass of fiery moths. Suddenly – with a loud *whumpph!* – the whole lot collapsed.

Almost everything I owned had been in that tent, but I didn't care about that. No, what I really wanted to know was where Wormrick and Jed were.

I dashed off to the stables. I prayed I'd find them both there, safe and sound. I elbowed my way through the crowd of knights and squires that had gathered to watch the fire, and burst in the doors of the stable.

"Wormrick!" I bellowed. "*Wormrick!*"

In front of me, there came a soft rustle from the corner of the stables, and a spotty face peered up at me from the straw.

"Oh, sir," he said as he stood up. "I've been

so worried. The duke sent a couple of his men to find you."

"I know," I said, smiling. "They gave me quite a warm welcome."

"I just grabbed what I could and came here," Wormrick went on. "First thing I did was to disguise Jed. That patched sur-coat of his is a bit of a give-away. So I swapped it for one from another horse, hid myself and waited. I didn't know what else to do."

"You did well, Wormrick," I said. "I'm proud of you."

Just then I felt hot breath on the back of my neck. I turned and saw Jed standing beside me, dressed in a black and silver sur-coat. I recognised it at once. It had belonged to the Rich Kid's war horse.

Maybe Jed sensed that the sur-coat belonged to a dead horse. Maybe all the fuss outside had unnerved him. Whatever, he was not his usual self. He was pawing at the ground, rolling his eyes and chomping at the bit.

"It's all right, Jed," I said, as I patted him on his neck. "Everything's all right."

Soon he was snorting down his nose into my face and licking my salty palms as if nothing at all had ever been the matter. Outside, the noise got louder. Jeers and whistles rose up above loud, angry voices.

"Wait here, Wormrick," I said. "I think our friends are back. Look after Jed. And make sure no one touches him."

I drew my sword a second time, headed for the stable doors and strode outside. A half-circle of faces greeted me, each one more ugly than the last. Ginger and Scar Face were among them, and in the middle of the line, Duke Wolfhound himself. His eyes narrowed in menace when he saw me.

"I thought we had a deal, sir knight," he hissed. He looked round and spoke to his henchmen. "It seems that these days you can't trust a knight to keep his promise – but then what can you expect from a free lance?"

"It takes two to honour a deal," I replied. "You didn't tell me about the war-lance when we made our little agreement," I said. My arm still throbbed at the memory.

"Ah, yes, that," said Duke Wolfhound. "I'm afraid Hengist got a little over-excited. He no longer works for me. And neither," he added, "do you. Guards!" he bellowed. "Seize him!"

The burly oafs came at me, their clubs and maces swinging.

Things weren't looking good. My throbbing arm was about to become the least of my worries.

"Stop wight there!" a voice cried.

It was the herald. He was buttoning up his tabard as he hurried towards us. His eyes fell upon Duke Wolfhound.

"So this is where you've got to, your Gwace," he said. "Shouldn't you be at the banquet with your guests?"

"Yes, yes," said the duke. "I have a small matter to clear up here first, Herald," he said. "I shan't be long."

The herald tut-tutted. "Your Gwace," he said, "if you have a

pwoblem with one of your knights, it is usual
to consult the hewald."

Duke Wolfhound looked flustered. "I ... I
didn't think ..." he began.

"That is the twouble," the herald said
sharply. "You didn't think!" He stepped

forward. "I am the hewald. I weport diwectly to the Gwand Tournament Council. If they were to hear of this, then your status as the host of a gwand tournament might well be at wisk."

"But … but …" the duke began.

"Never mind your 'buts'," the herald said. "There have been a number of complaints at this tournament alweady. Horses acting oddly. Large bets placed on complete outsiders," he went on. He looked hard at Duke Wolfhound. "I have also noticed that a tent has burned down."

Ginger and Scar Face looked down at their boots.

"And now I find a knight about to be hurt," the herald cried. "I won't have it! Not at a tournament of which I am the hewald! Call off your men, your Gwace, or the next tournament you'll host will be on nothing more than a village gween! I twust I make myself clear."

Duke Wolfhound scowled. "Yes," he snarled, and he clicked his fingers.

His henchmen backed off, and the whole lot of them slunk away. I turned to the herald. "Thank you," I said.

"Don't thank me, Fwee Lance," he said in a sharp voice. "Knights like you attwact twouble. You don't belong in a major tournament. But, as you're here, it is my duty to make sure you follow the wules to the letter!"

With that, he turned on his heels and strode off. I watched him go. He was a stickler for the rules, but that was exactly the kind of person I needed to make it to the end of the tournament alive. After that, I'd be on my own.

I went back to the stables. It was warm inside after the chill wind outside, and the straw smelled sweet and inviting. I slumped down, curled up and closed my eyes ... The next thing I knew, Wormrick was shaking me awake.

"I've rubbed down Jed and polished your armour, sir," he said. "And her ladyship has sent a tray of eggs from the castle kitchens for your breakfast."

Duke Wolfhound hadn't finished with me yet. I knew I'd need more than a tray of eggs to get me to the end of the long day ahead.

I had yet to discover just how long that day would be.

7

A trumpet blast rang out around the soggy tournament field. The excited crowd fell silent and all eyes fell on the herald, who strode forward, his boots sinking into the mud with every step. The heavy morning rain had given way to endless drizzle and I was wet and cold.

At the far end of the field, I saw the Blue Knight climb into the saddle. Beneath me, Jed trembled.

"What's up, boy?" I whispered. The trumpet blast would always make him paw the ground and chomp at the bit, but not today. No, today Jed was slow, yet nervy, and had hardly touched his breakfast, even though Wormrick had served him up the finest oat-mash the castle had to offer.

"Everything all right, sir?" came a voice, and I turned to see Wormrick standing beside us, my lance in his hands.

"I'm worried about Jed," I told him. "Are you sure none of the duke's men has got to him?"

"They couldn't have, sir. I was with him all evening. I'd have spotted any funny business." He paused. "Mind you, there was one thing ..."

"Yes?" I said.

"No, it's nothing, sir."

"Tell me, Wormrick."

"Well," he said, and he looked puzzled. "It was that lady."

"What lady?"

"Her ladyship's maid," he said. "You know, the one with the black hair."

"What about her?" I asked.

"It's just that when I first got to the stables, she was there. With Jed. She was patting him and whispering into his ear. She was ever so gentle. Said she loved horses, sir, and that Jed was a very fine animal," he added. "So I didn't see any harm in it, sir."

"No, Wormrick," I said. "I'm sure there wasn't."

"Look," said Wormrick, pointing. "There she is now, sir, staring at Jed. Can't keep her eyes off him."

I turned, looked up at the grandstand – and straight into the eyes of the dark-haired maid. A thin smile danced on her lips.

I shivered. I had a bad feeling about this, a really bad feeling.

In front of her sat her ladyship, next to Duke Wolfhound.

A second trumpet blast rang out, and her ladyship stood up. Her face was as white as a sheet and she was all a-tremble.

The Blue Knight had taken his lance from his squire, and was holding it like an old lady with a walking stick.

The herald raised his hand. "Ladies and gentlemen," he cried. "The Gwand Final!"

A loud cheer went up. The herald turned to the grandstand. "If your ladyship would be so kind."

Her ladyship fumbled with the silk purse in her hands. Her face was ashen. The duke scowled and nudged her, and I saw him lift his hand so no one could see what he hissed at her.

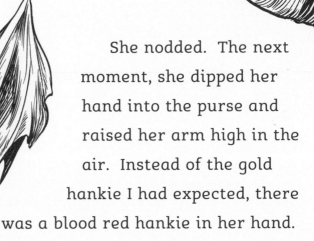

She nodded. The next moment, she dipped her hand into the purse and raised her arm high in the air. Instead of the gold hankie I had expected, there was a blood red hankie in her hand.

The crowd gasped. Even the herald looked shocked.

"Are you quite sure, your ladyship?" he asked.

"Of course she's sure," Duke Wolfhound answered for her. "As Queen of the Tournament Field, she has every right." He rested his hand heavily on her arm. "Let it go," he snarled.

Tears streamed down her cheeks as her ladyship let the hankie drop. It fluttered to the ground like a dying sparrow. The herald stepped forward.

"A field-of-blood joust," he declared, his voice shaky. "A fight to the death."

I shook my head. So this was what Duke Wolfhound had planned. He was clever. As clever as the devil, in fact. If the Blue Knight killed me, then the duke would have got his revenge. But if I beat the Blue Knight, I'd have to kill him to claim my prize. Duke Wolfhound didn't think I had the guts to do it, which meant he wouldn't have to pay out any prize money. Whatever happened now, he would win.

'Life in the Majors!' I thought with a shudder. It might look grand from the outside, but inside it was rotten.

"Let the field-of-blood joust begin!" the herald cried.

I turned to Wormrick. "May as well get this over with," I said. "Wish me luck!"

The trumpet sounded a third time, and I twitched Jed's reins. He didn't move. From the grandstand, I could feel the raven-haired maid's gaze on us, like the eyes of a hawk on its prey.

"Come on, Jed," I urged. "Don't let me down, not now ..."

All at once, Jed lurched forward and picked up speed, as he galloped over the spongy ground. The Blue Knight galloped towards me, flapping about like a fat abbot on a donkey, his lance all over the place. I couldn't miss.

I really hated to do this to him, whoever he was – but I had no choice. It was him or me. I lowered my lance into position.

All of a sudden I felt a terrible shudder
shake Jed's body from head to tail. He arched
his back, then crashed into the muddy field,
sending me flying through the air. The ground
rushed up to meet me. The next thing I knew,
there was a roar in my ears and I could see
stars.

There was mud everywhere – in my eyes, my mouth. It tasted foul. I spat it out as I scrambled to my feet.

From behind me, I could hear the pounding of hoofs. I spun round. The Blue Knight was bearing down on me, a great studded club in his hand. Before I could react, the club struck me and I went down for a second time.

I could hear the crowd screaming and shouting and calling for blood. I rolled over. The Blue Knight had got off his horse. His club lay on the ground behind him. In his hands was a heavy broadsword which hissed through the air as he came to finish me off.

There was blood in my mouth, the sun in my eyes … I had never thought it would end like this.

The Blue Knight stood over me and lifted his sword above his head, ready to stab it into my heart. He was so close I could see his blue eyes twinkling from behind his visor. *Too* close …

With every last ounce of strength, I kicked out and took the knight's legs out from under him. It was his turn to come crashing to the ground. I was on my feet in an instant, and on him, my sword at his throat.

The crowd roared with delight.

... to the death ... to the death – the herald's words were an echo inside my head.

Just then, I heard a screech from the grandstand. I looked round to see the raven-haired maid racing towards me, her nails drawn, her teeth bared and her thick black hair streaming behind her.

"*No!*" she screamed. "*NO!*"

Two men-at-arms leaped forward and pulled her back.

"No! No!" she cried. "I won't let you kill him!"

A murmur went round the crowd.

I looked up at Duke Wolfhound. He sneered back at me. "It's a field of blood, Free Lance!"

He smiled, his evil fangs glinting. "You will have to kill him if you want your money."

The herald confirmed that the duke was right. "Wules are wules," he murmured with a nod.

"I won't kill a man without seeing his face," I said and drew my sword back. "Take off your helmet."

The Blue Knight did as he was told. And there, staring back at me, was the handsome face of the troubadour.

From the grandstand, her ladyship screamed and jumped up from her seat.

"What are you waiting for, sir knight?" the troubadour said, his voice bitter. "Go on. Finish me off …"

"No! No!" the maid screeched, as she struggled to get free from the men-at-arms. "Don't listen to him, Free Lance. Anybody

can see that he is no knight. He's just a poor
troubadour. He doesn't deserve to die. It
was *I* who cast a spell on your horse, and
all the other horses, so that the troubadour
would win the tournament. And then we'd be
rich enough to get married and give up this
wandering life ..."

"Married?" her ladyship cried from the grandstand. "But he loves *me*!"

"Loves you?" The maid glared at her ladyship. "He could never love a pampered princess like you. You were just a plaything. He told me so."

Her ladyship stared at the troubadour. He smiled, his face cruel.

"It was fun while it lasted," he said. "But now it's over. What are you waiting for, Free Lance?"

"You heard the scum," Duke Wolfhound sneered. "He's only a troubadour. He won't be missed." He laughed when I did not move. "Just as I suspected. Our brave Free Lance here hasn't the stomach for a field of blood. My money is safe!"

The herald stepped forward. "It is unfortunate," he said, "but there is nothing

I can do. A field of blood is a field of blood.
Either finish him off, Fwee Lance, or lose the
prize."

I looked around. Her ladyship was sobbing,
Duke Wolfhound was sneering, the maid had
her head in her hands. As for the troubadour,
he was glaring at me.

"Kill! Kill!" cried some voices from the
crowd, and soon the chant went up – "Kill! Kill!
Kill!"

I raised my sword – and then put it away.

I looked round at the jeering faces, as the chants gave way to cat-calls and boos. And at that moment, I knew I'd had it with the Major Tournaments. From now on, I'd stick to the manor-house tournaments and to the village greens.

"You all disgust me," I said, and I spat on the ground as I turned and walked away from the tournament field.

Jed trotted up to me as if nothing had happened, with Wormrick running behind him. It was good to see them. I couldn't wait to get away – but first, there was one last thing I had to do.

*

"Thank you, thank you, brave sir knight," her ladyship said, a bright sparkle in her emerald eyes. "I don't know how I can ever repay you."

"I'm just glad to have been of help," I said.

"Oh, you have," she cried. "Without you, I would never have got away from my wicked uncle." She looked around. "And I'm sure I'll be happy here. They're good people."

I nodded. She was right. They might not be able to joust, but the east country noblemen had kind hearts.

We were standing in front of the manor house of one of her distant cousins, and as her ladyship waved goodbye, I knew that I'd left her in good hands. I'd given her the thirty gold coins that Duke Wolfhound had given me as a bribe at the start. She'd be able to hire a maid she could trust.

The raven-haired maid had been drummed out of town with that troubadour boyfriend of hers. As for Duke Wolfhound, he'd saved the prize money and the herald had promised me he wouldn't report him to the Grand Tournament Council. In return, the duke had let her ladyship go. If he was ashamed of making her drop the red hankie, he showed no sign of it.

I sighed. I might not have won the winner's purse, but at least I had no blood on my hands. And one good thing had come out of the whole adventure – now I had a faithful squire.

"Where to now, sir?" Wormrick asked as we galloped off.

"I've no idea," I said.

"Sir?" he said, looking confused.

"You are a squire to a free lance now, Wormrick," I said. "I can't promise you riches, or soft beds, or a warm fire to sit beside – but there's one thing I can give you in plenty."

"What's that?" Wormrick asked, his voice deep and steady.

"Adventure," I said.